THE HUNTING GROUND

Lise Tremblay

Translated by Linda Gaboriau

Talonbooks
Vancouver

Talonbooks
P.O. Box 2076, Vancouver, British Columbia, Canada V6B 3S3
www.talonbooks.com

Typeset in Mrs. Eaves and printed and bound in Canada.

First Printing: 2006

The publisher gratefully acknowledges the financial support of the Canada Council for the Arts; the Government of Canada through the Book Publishing Industry Development Program; and the Province of British Columbia through the British Columbia Arts Council for our publishing activities.

La héronnière by Lise Tremblay was first published in French by Leméac Éditeur Inc., Montreal. Financial support for this translation provided by the Canada Council for the Arts and the Department of Canadian Heritage through the Book Publishing Industry Development Program.

LIBRARY AND ARCHIVES CANADA CATALOGUING IN PUBLICATION

Tremblay, Lise, 1957–
[Héronnière. English]
The hunting ground / Lise Tremblay ; translated by Linda Gaboriau.

Translation of: La héronnière.
ISBN 0-88922-534-6

I. Gaboriau, Linda II. Title.

PS8589.R4465H4713 2006 C843'.54 C2005-906203-7

ISBN-10: 0-88922-534-6
ISBN-13: 978-0-88922-534-3

Many thanks to Alexandra Bolduc for her important contribution to this book.

Contents

… and the herons' throats
sing in soft fluted sounds under the knife …

—Karel Jan Čapek, "Les Morts à la chasse"

The Trailer

"THE TRAILER." Now that she's gone, I repeat these words every time I come home from the hunting camp and pull into the driveway. As soon as we built the extension, Nicole started saying "the house" and if I happened to say the trailer, she'd sulk. Like she was ashamed.

The first two summers we lived there, she spent all her time in the yard sowing flowers and planting shrubs. She had me transplant some fir trees that I placed along the driveway and at the corners of the house. She'd drawn a plan on a page from our accounts book. The trees in the corners had to be placed in a triangle, and in the middle we planted some weeping birches that I went to get in the city and they cost me two days' salary. I said it was expensive. She didn't answer. Today, the front of the trailer has practically disappeared behind the foliage and from the road, you would never guess it's a mobile home.

In late June, when the roses are in bloom, the tourists are always at the door, asking permission to take pictures of the rose garden near the porch. Rose garden, it sounds so fancy. That's what Nicole started calling it when we had to get out the burlap bags to protect the bushes from the cold. It went on for years. The garden was her whole life. She ordered thick catalogues and pored over them during the winter. She always kept the same plan. The paper got yellowed and dirty, she added notes in red. The women in the village came to consult her about their yards. Whenever people talked about flowers, I'd hear them say, "We should ask Nicole." She'd become a kind of expert. We had our daughters. She took good care of them, but I always noticed that she worried more about her flowers. One summer there was a tornado. One of her silver maples fell on her hedge. She cried for two days. It's one of the only times I saw her so upset. It's a strange thing to say, but it's true.

Before long the girls went off to school. The first few years I had to go to pick them up at the bus station in the neighbouring town, it was two hundred kilometres round trip, every weekend. They'd arrive with their suitcases full of dirty laundry and they'd leave on Sunday with the spaghetti sauce and canned meat Nicole had prepared in advance. Then they stopped coming so often, and for years now I've only seen them at Christmas and Easter. They sleep for four days straight and leave saying the village is the most boring place on earth. I don't answer. I don't talk much in general. I'm not a talker. It's one of the things she always complained about. Personally, I didn't see what there was to say. I was in charge of the hunting camp, I had a decent salary and the girls were doing well at school. She had her garden and was active in the choir and the altar guild at the church. Those evenings I'd go watch the game at Léon's. He was the first one to get a satellite dish. Léon learned to speak English in British Columbia. He lived out there for five years before coming back to take over his father's grocery store. Everyone was surprised. We thought he'd left for good. There were four or five of us who'd get together to nurse a beer and watch the game in English. Every so often, Léon would translate part of the interviews with the players, but hockey is hockey, in English or in French. With satellite, there was a game on almost every night.

By the end of this hunting season, it will have been two years since she left. We were married for twenty-eight years. I was fifteen years older than her, but we weren't the only ones like that here in the village. When I'm not at the hunting camp, I spend my time driving around the back roads. I can't stay in the trailer more than two hours in a row. I suffocate. So I drive around, I put the music on as loud as I can, like the teenagers do, and I force myself not to think. That's why I can't stay in the trailer, I can't even watch TV, I start thinking. I ask myself how it all started. At one point, she ordered me some fancier clothes from a catalogue and she made me change on Saturdays and Sundays. I thought I looked stupid, so I wouldn't leave the house. I was afraid the guys in town would make fun of me. I was dressed like the tourists who come in the summer, with their funny colours: beige, pale blue, women's colours. I did it so she wouldn't sulk. Sometimes she'd sulk for two, three days, but that wasn't a sign because she'd always done that, even when we first got married. I hate thinking about it, my head gets all fuzzy.

A couple of years ago, Nicole decided to open a tourist stand at the entrance to the village. She rented the old abandoned snack bar and she had me paint it pink and mauve. I didn't like the colours but I admit you couldn't miss it. I always thought she got the idea from her girlfriend from the city. I never knew her name. She and her husband rent a house year round, just down the road at the turnoff to the big lake. At first, she just came to the house to buy bread and paté. She was a good customer, and she brought other business. When I got home from the camp, I'd often find them sitting together in the porch swing. The other one would always excuse herself and leave right away. I thought she was polite.

Over the winter, Nicole made all sorts of things for her stand: flowery hats to hang on doors, faceless dolls that were seen from the back and looked like they were always crying. She even took some of the carved pheasants and ducks my brother-in-law made in his shed and that she had forbidden me to put in our living room. She said that to us he was just a whittler, but the tourists were willing to pay big bucks for that stuff. I found out from my sister that her friend from the city had bought three of them and she'd paid twice the price my brother-in-law asked. The stand kept her busy. I could spend my time at Léon's, and she no longer complained. I probably should have suspected something. I thought that I'd married her when she was young and now she'd grown older. Nicole had just turned forty-five. She had her business and she took care of the parish church. She even offered to come to the hunting club in the fall to help the cook. She'd developed a taste for money, that's what I thought.

I didn't see that that woman was always stopping by to visit her. I might have suspected something. She never said anything in front of me, she was always polite. She'd sent me some customers for the hunting club and summer tenants for the old house on Boulder Road. She knew a lot of people. Once we even saw her on television. She was talking about the history of the villages in the region. She seemed to know a lot on the subject. My brother-in-law told me it was her fault that Nicole left, that she'd put ideas in her head. That's what he told me recently. He and my sister had heard talk around town. Everyone knows it's no good to let strangers get too close. Those friendships always end badly. I don't know how many examples there's been in the village.

But I didn't notice a thing. Actually, things had never been better. Nicole would come to the hunting camp, we were working twelve hours a day and putting some money aside. She gave me half of her pay. We had savings. We were even thinking of spending part of the winter in Florida like her brother did. She said we could rent a trailer in the same park and we could learn to play golf. I didn't notice a thing.

The following year, she didn't come home one night in the fall. I thought she must've slept at the employees' cabin because she had too much work. That had happened before, especially those times when we only had twenty-four hours for the changeover between hunting parties. I hadn't seen her for two days, I'd gone to the city for supplies. The next morning when I stopped to get gas, Léon asked me to come in for a few minutes, into his house, not the grocery store. His wife put some coffee down on the table and left the kitchen. I was scared. I knew he was going to announce some bad news. It was the second time he'd invited me in like that. The first time was the day my brother Sylvain drowned. No one ever knew how, but he fell out of his rowboat. Léon was fishing with some other guys on the big lake that day. They weren't aware of anything, but when they came back at the end of the day, they found the empty rowboat with the fishing rod still in the bow. The divers brought him up the following day. It took less than two hours. The police said, "He's intact, not swollen, nothing." I was the one who identified the body. They opened the bag down to his chin. It was true, he was intact. He hadn't even turned twenty. That time, too, I'd gone into the city for the hunting camp. Léon's the one who broke the news to me when I got back.

He waited until I sat down and he said, "There's worse than what I've got to tell you, for sure, when Sylvain died it was worse, but, last night, Nicole came to the store with a hunter, she got out of the car and they were kissing the whole time I was filling the tank. He's at the lodge and he hasn't gone hunting for the past two days. He waits for her to finish her work and they go walking around the cottages, holding hands. The whole village knows. She's not even trying to hide it. I wanted to tell you. I think you have to be reasonable."

For sure it wasn't as bad as my brother, but it was a blow. On top of everything, it was my first year as general manager. I'd even had supper with the owners. I couldn't settle my score with the guy without risking my job.

She left the following day. She only took her clothes. She didn't ask me for anything, no alimony, not even her half of the house, or the furniture. She even left her aunt's old sideboard that's supposed to be worth a fortune. She told the girls to keep coming to see me, that I was a good man. I didn't like that. What does that mean, *a good man*? A pushover? A dummy? A hick?

I thought she'd want a divorce but she's never mentioned it. I've run into her two or three times on the road coming into the village. It's always the same thing. She waves for me to stop. She pulls over to the side of the road and comes to talk to me through the window of my truck, leaning her arms on the edge of the window. It's funny because in all the years we spent together, we always talked like that. She stays there for a long time and he sits waiting in the car. She asks about my sister, her nephews, the hunting camp. Once she's gone through the list, she stops and tells me about the girls and how she sees them more often now that she's living in Montreal, but not as often as she'd like, mostly she talks to them on the phone. She says everyone's always in a hurry in the city. She works six months of the year in a nursery. She always says what she misses most is the view of the lake we had from the house, and her rose garden. She only comes back to the village to see her father, and not very often. He's mad at her for leaving. At first, he called her every name in the book. Lately, he's calmed down, mostly because it upset the girls. She never stays long. Not long enough to see her friends. Not one of them has heard from her since she left. My sister always says, "It's like she died." The first year Nicole didn't even answer her Christmas card. I know she can't forgive her. Once she called and Nicole answered, yes, no, like she was pulling teeth. But back here in the village, they were inseparable. Thirty years of friendship. Then, nothing.

When I saw her again for the first time, I didn't recognize her. It's strange because she hasn't changed, at least, not physically. Afterwards, I thought it was because she looked like the tourists. She acts like them. It's hard to say if it's arrogance or embarrassment. I try not to think about it. I spend more time at the hunting camp. I feed the wild turkeys even in the winter. At night, I drive around in my truck listening to Johnny Cash.

Once I happened to see a show about his life. I'd never heard anyone sing like that. I had Léon order me two tapes. I didn't regret it. He's all I listen to now.

Actually, I think Nicole was influenced. I don't know what that woman put into her head. She didn't look like much, so polite. She had a strange way of dressing and it was her husband who took care of the house. I'm not sure I'd even recognize him. He acts like a woman, does all the cooking and never goes out. They still come to the village. They finally bought a house on Hemlock Road. She often visits one of my cousins. Maybe they should be careful. I don't like thinking about it too much. I can still see her at the shop, friendly, polite, always smiling, talking in her quiet voice. She'd leave as soon as I arrived, she didn't want to bother us.

A schemer.

I don't know what she told Nicole. Sometimes I think none of this would have happened if that woman had stayed home. Too sweet, that's how she looked, with her fancy dresses. During the summer I drive by their house every night in my truck. I can't help it. I know their habits. They live by candlelight, like in the old days. They sit around a big table on the porch. They often have guests. They stay there till late at night. Sometimes, I get these crazy ideas, I scare myself. I think of how surprised they'd be if one night I stopped, just like that. I'd leave the door to my truck open so I could hear Johnny Cash. I'd take out my hunting rifle, not my shotgun for ducks, no, the other one, the big one, for moose, the rifle I gave to my brother Sylvain.

The Heron Colony

THAT THURSDAY, I was the one who picked up the dead birds. When I saw the two herons and the pintails floating near the shore of the lake, I stopped my truck. They weren't there the day before, I was sure of that. I go by there every day and I often stop to watch the herons fishing. Their colony is over in the marsh, about ten miles away at the foot of the mountain.

I've known where it is since I was a kid. We never went there because it smelled too bad and we used to call it the ghost swamp. It really is a strange place. First of all, there's the marsh full of mosquitoes, then you have to walk through the muck and the bird droppings. The place is full of dead fir trees, still standing bare, their feet buried under the skeletons of the baby herons. Twice a year, the biologists come to visit the heronry. I'd never heard that word before I met them, it sounds so serious. I'm the one who drives them there because I know those back roads. But I don't go in with them, I can't stand the smell. I wait in my truck. Usually there are two of them, a young guy and the old man. They gather bones, feathers, droppings. It's always the same old guy, I've known him for twenty years. The first time I mentioned the heron colony to him, we were down at little Drouin Lake and he was catching frogs. We'd just seen a great heron fly away. I said, "I bet he's going back to the nesting ground at the foot of the mountain." He asked me,

"You know where it is?" I nodded and he started jumping up and down and shouting. Like a madman. At the time I didn't realize how rare it was. Now, every time I stop by the lake, I think of him.

And I was thinking of him as I walked over to the dead birds. I thought they might have been poisoned and that I should send him a message. We stay in touch, as he says. When my daughter hooked me up to the Internet on the computer, I sent him a message. He answered the next day. He was glad I was "on line." He wrote that I'd get into it and the winter wouldn't seem so long. We write to each other regularly, especially about clearing the ponds around the camp. I walked to the edge of the water and I flipped one of the herons over with a stick. It was riddled with bullets—not buckshot, but bullets. The three other birds were in the same state, shot right in the heart, just beneath the wings. I knew who had killed them. There was only one guy in the village who was such a good shot. But he'd never killed any birds outside of the hunting season, let alone herons. He knew they were one of the endangered species.

He's been following me around for the past ten years. Besides the fact that he tends to fill the ducks with buckshot—I've had to tell him not to because the hunters don't like it—he's a good worker and at seventeen, he's the best hunting guide in the whole region. And he's an ace trainer, his dogs win all the competitions. Our village is well-known because of him. But this time, I thought, Steeve was getting out of hand.

I figured a lot of people must have seen the dead birds because the little lake is right at the entrance to town. I went back to my truck and got my spade. Once spring arrives, I always have my tools with me. I fished the birds out of the water and buried them one by one. We had two days left before the opening of the Birdwatchers Symposium. The village was about to be invaded by a hundred tourists equipped with binoculars and telescopes powerful enough for them to see the eagles on the mountain. Our reputation was at stake, they'd better not see endangered birds massacred in the middle of our ponds.

Ever since this Symposium has existed, I have to admit, even though I'm not crazy about tourists, it's brought a lot of money to town. During that weekend, all the lodges and the rented rooms are always full and people have started to come from all around the province. Lots of them come back during the summer for cycling and birdwatching. Hunting is no longer enough. The mayor keeps reminding us, "No more tourists, no more village."

I got back into my truck and instead of going straight to the camp, I came back to the house. Something told me Steeve had gone on a rampage and I took the ATV and went to check the other ponds. I put a net and a shovel in my trailer. Steeve had made the rounds before me. I found three or four birds in every pond. I buried them all. He'd even shot down crows along the paths. He'd gone beserk. It took me most of the afternoon.

I was beside myself. My job was at stake. Outside the hunting season, I was supposed to protect the hunting camp, keep an eye on all the comings and goings, clear the brush, prevent poaching. If one of the owners showed up, I'd be out of work.

I didn't stop for lunch, I wasn't hungry. I was too furious. I had only one thing on my mind. I wanted to back Steeve up against a wall and punch him in the face. I was fit to be tied all afternoon. On my way home, I saw him at the grocery store, loading a case of beer into the back of his old van. He was with some other young guys from town. He gave me a big wave. I pretended not to see him, didn't wave or nod. I drove by without turning my head.

I went home. I took a shower and ate a bowl of cereal and drank a cup of instant decaf coffee. I didn't feel like going for a beer at Léon's, the way I do almost every night. I sat down in front of the TV and I must've dozed off for a while. Around eleven o'clock, after the news, I went to bed. I was incapable of falling back to sleep. I was still furious. I could only hope that not many people had seen the dead birds and that no one would mention it during the Symposium. I couldn't tell anyone, I didn't want to let the cat out of the bag. I'd have to catch up with Steeve early the next morning to prevent him from continuing his killing spree. That kid was starting to worry me.

Last fall he refused to go back to school. He spent the winter cooped up, watching television and playing video games. He didn't even want to come snowmobiling with us. I went to get him twice and both times he refused, hardly looking at me. He was alone in the house. He didn't even help his father cut the wood.

His mother, like every winter, was busy preparing for the Symposium at what's-his-face Lefebvre's house. Once she called me in tears. My brother-in-law had had a fight with Steeve and it almost got out of hand. Steeve had gone on a binge the night before and driven the Jeep into a ditch. It was badly damaged. He was blind drunk. My brother-in-law would have to pay for the repairs to avoid an investigation by his insurance company. I told her not to worry, that we'd all done things like that when we were young, and it was just a phase. She wanted me to talk to him. I was his uncle and he'd always trusted me. So I said okay, I'd do it, first chance I got.

Every February, they organize a kind of carnival here, with a contest for princesses and a coronation. There's a big party. People from all around attend. Steeve was there with his friends, and I went over to see him. He wasn't acting his usual self and I thought he'd smoked a joint or two with his buddies. I asked him how things were going at home and right away he said his mother wasn't around much. It was strange, she was the one he was mad at. I asked him some questions, but I couldn't get him to say what she had done to upset him. He told me this was the last winter he'd be spending in the village, that was for sure, he was going to work in his uncle's convenience store in Quebec City. I told him several times he should watch his behaviour and he said "Yes, Uncle" in a little boy's voice to make fun of me, then he put his hand on my shoulder and offered me a beer. I could feel that he was hiding something from me but I couldn't tell what.

Friday morning, I saw dawn come peeking through the curtains. At seven, the alarm rang and I got up. I ate breakfast fast and left for the village. I slowed down in front of Nancy's house. I could see that she was up and I stopped. She was sitting at the kitchen table organizing some brochures. She came to let me in. She was wearing the official Symposium t-shirt. The design showed a Great Blue Heron in flight, one of Roger Lefebvre's ideas. She offered me a cup of coffee and I said yes. I didn't want to look like I was in a hurry. She came over to the table to show me a strange-looking coffee pot Roger had bought for her in the city. She couldn't say two sentences without mentioning Roger-this, Roger-that. It was annoying.

I drank my coffee and let her tell me all the ins and outs of organizing the Symposium and how the mayor had exploited them and their work, how he continued to exploit them. I let her talk. When I got up to leave, I said I wanted to have a word with Steeve about the hunting camp. She pointed to the stairs to the basement and grumbled, "He came home late."

The bedroom stank of alcohol and sweat. Steeve was sleeping on his stomach, his mouth open. He'd gained an awful lot of weight in the past year. I shook him.

"Wake up."

He sat up in the middle of his bed.

"Can you tell me what came over you? Are you crazy? Two days before the Symposium. You're going to make us look like savages."

He squinted at me.

"What are you talking about?"

"You know what I'm talking about. Why did you go around shooting like that?"

"I wasn't the only one."

"That's no excuse."

He lay back down and turned his head to the wall.

"Don't pretend you're sleeping. You're going to lay off immediately, or you can forget your job at the hunting camp."

"I don't give a shit."

"If you keep it up, I'm going to turn you in. I need to earn a living. I'm not going to let you make me lose my job. You hear me?"

He grunted. I left the room, madder than ever. The kid wasn't himself. I figured I'd wait till the Symposium was over and then I'd come have a talk with his mother. Something was going on and I couldn't put my finger on it. I wasn't so sure he wouldn't start again. I'd turned in poachers before and I wasn't afraid to do it again. Steeve was my nephew, but I wasn't going to sit back and let him ruin everything.

That evening, the tourists began to arrive. My sister and Roger Lefebvre greeted them at the entrance to the village at a stand shaped like a duck's head. I couldn't get the sight of the dead birds out of my mind. I stopped by everywhere, the garage, the grocery store, the bar. I wanted to know if anyone had seen the dead birds or seen him shooting. At the grocery store, Léon said Steeve was really carrying on these days. I realized he knew. I told him that had been settled. But Léon wouldn't say a word to anybody, partly because he's my cousin and we grew up together, and partly because that's how Léon is. He doesn't go around repeating everything he hears and sees in the village. That's how he manages to keep his customers. The grocery stores in the neighbouring villages closed down ages ago and people have to drive a hundred kilometres a week to buy a bag of apples.

Léon is a survivor, and my best friend. His wife left him for a stranger, too. She did it a long time before mine did.

He met another woman through an ad, and she's been with him, working with him in the grocery store, for over fifteen years now. She's no Brigitte Bardot, but she's a good sort. When my wife left with a hunter she'd known for a week, if Léon hadn't been there, I don't know what I would have done. He didn't say much, but he always offered me a beer at the beginning of the games we watched together, and when I was leaving, he always said, "I'll be expecting you tomorrow night, you owe me one." That lasted for the whole first winter. In the spring, when I started to work again, he told me, "The worst is over. The first winter is awful, when the village is pretty much dead and everyone's watching to see how you'll react and they've got nothing better to do than watch you." He was right. In the spring, I felt a lot better.

I spent all day Saturday between the grocery store and the garage, watching the birdwatchers wander through town. They all look the same: camouflage outfits, backpacks, all kinds of binoculars hanging around their necks or over their shoulders. The women all look alike, too. This is no Miss World contest: no makeup, their hair in braids or pulled back in a pony tail, no dye. I don't know why, almost all of them have grey hair and wear glasses. Around four o'clock, they headed for the woods. And we wouldn't see them again till seven or eight at the bird call contest.

I went home to get ready. The contest is my favourite activity. It takes place after the traditional country supper in the big reception room at the hotel. Everyone goes. For an hour straight, you see doctors, engineers, important people go up on the stage and try to imitate bird calls, making faces you wouldn't believe. And the thing I find most hilarious is that this is the most serious contest I've ever seen. There's dead silence during the performances. It's always the best night of my year. I've even convinced Léon to come with me. He's a guy who never leaves his store for more than ten minutes, but now he wouldn't miss the contest for anything in the world.

We had supper, Léon and me and his wife, with a couple from Quebec City who'd already been here last year. They talked about the number of dying villages, about the rural exodus and the need for eco-tourism. It was pretty depressing. Like one of the mayor's round robin letters. We'd finished eating long before the contest began. I couldn't understand why they were starting so late. Finally my sister came to the mic. Léon and I were really surprised, she's usually so shy. She handled it really well. The lineup of participants began. When it was over, when they gave out the prizes, I realized I hadn't seen Roger Lefebvre all evening. That was surprising. He usually plays emcee and Nancy distributes the trophies. I had one last beer with Léon and I left the hotel.

That's when I heard Nancy calling me. She was upset, I could tell from the way she was walking. When she caught up with me, she said, "I want you to come with me to Roger's place. There's something wrong. He's not answering his phone at home or his cell phone. Something's happened to him, I'm sure. At four, he went to change and rest a bit, he never came back." She went back to her Jeep and I followed her. Lefebvre's cabin is five miles north of the village. You have to know where the turnoff is, otherwise it's impossible to find. We've always called the place "the cabin on the outskirts" even though it's become a house now. Roger Lefebvre bought it about ten years ago and he renovated it. It's the only house on the river, it's isolated, with no one around for miles.

I've never understood what Nancy saw in the guy, besides the fact that he used big words and he memorized the names of hundreds of species of birds. If you ask me, for a stranger, he took up a lot of space in our village. And nobody knows the truth about his past. At first, people said he was a retired teacher, then at one point, I heard he'd been a technician with Hydro Québec. No one from his family ever came to visit. His only visitors were his birdwatcher friends. The Symposium was his idea.

The first year Nancy worked with him, it set tongues wagging in the village. I was sure it was just gossip, that there was nothing between him and her. My sister was still young and so was her husband. And old man Lefebvre had to be over sixty, and he wasn't what you'd call handsome. He was short and had tiny hands and strange, bulging eyes. Not very appetizing. Over the years, people stopped talking. At least, I never heard tell of it again. My sister helped organize the Symposium as a pastime. The women in the village don't have much to do, aside from working for the tourists and taking care of the church, and they get bored, especially when their kids grow up. A lot of them have left because of that. But in a small town, people talk. You get used to it or you leave.

I was following the Jeep. Nancy was driving fast, holding her cell phone to her ear. She must've been trying to reach him. At the turnoff, I lost sight of her behind the spruce trees. She'd sped up even more. She arrived a bit before me. Roger Lefebvre's van was parked there, with the headlights on. The light on the porch lit up the front of the house, all the way to the water. My sister parked her Jeep just behind the van. I saw her get out and walk around his car. At one point, she stopped. I ran over to her. At first I didn't see anything, then I saw Roger Lefebvre's body lying face down. Blood had splattered the door of his van.

I don't know how long we stood there without saying a thing, maybe two, three minutes. I was the one who spoke first. It just came out. I said, "Someone shot old man Lefebvre." Nancy took my hand. We walked back to her Jeep. She dialled 911 and after repeating, yes, he was dead, three times, the receptionist transferred her to a policeman. She told him what we had just discovered. She passed me the phone, she was incapable of explaining how to get to the cabin. I gave the instructions and added that we'd wait for them at the turnoff. Twice he told us not to touch a thing, just wait. He forgot to hang up and we heard him tell someone, "Just my luck, a murder, for Chrissakes!"

We got back into my truck and drove to the corner of the road. It was late May and the nights were still cool. Nancy was shivering, I turned on the heater and took a bottle of Seven-Up from under my seat. I gave her some. She cried for a while silently. We decided to wait for the police before calling anyone. No point in getting the whole village up in arms right away. There'd be enough of an uproar as it was. At one point she wanted to go back to her Jeep to get her purse. I said no. I was afraid we'd miss the police car. She blew her nose on a rag I passed her. She complained she had a stomach ache. She got out to walk around and I saw her throw up, leaning with both hands on a tree. She asked me for another Seven-Up to rinse her mouth. She was shivering.

We waited for more than an hour. Nancy spent the whole time getting in and out of the truck. She felt sick to her stomach. I don't know why but I felt uncomfortable. I didn't know what to say to her. I could hardly wait for the police to arrive so I could go home and wash up.

Finally, I saw the ambulance headed our way. There were no flashing lights, no siren. The police followed in two cars. They stopped beside us and had us get into the back seat. I heard the doors click locked. I didn't like the sound.

They took a bunch of pictures with a flash, then they picked up the body. They questioned us separately. Nancy talked to them longer. I waited so I could take her home, she was in no state to drive her Jeep. We drove back in silence. She'd stopped crying. Every so often, she got the shivers. The cab of the truck was overheated, I could hardly breathe. My brother-in-law was in the kitchen. He came out when he saw me pull into the driveway. Nancy ran over to him. She didn't talk to him for long. She ran into the house and turned off the lights and drew the curtains. He came to see me. He was starting to get worried. He thought Nancy had had an accident. I told him the whole story. I said I'd stop by the next day. He shook my hand. That was strange.

I remember driving around for a while in the sleeping village. I don't know why, but hunting scenes kept going through my head. I was always the first one to approach the moose the hunters had killed. I was used to dead bodies.

The only words that came to mind were *nothing* and *dirty*. When I saw Roger Lefebvre's body, that's what I thought. That's what death was: nothing and dirty. I went home and took a shower. A long one.

Sunday was not a day like any other. It felt like a lost day, with no borders, no signposts. Léon told me the village woke up to five patrol cars parked in front of the community centre. Before long the whole town was gathered in the parking lot. People were waiting in their cars. I woke up late. It must've been eleven o'clock when I arrived at Léon's. He was waiting for me. He knew that I had found Roger Lefebvre's body with Nancy. We walked over to the community centre together.

At one point, the mayor came out onto the porch with Officer Girard. Everyone knows him. He's the police officer in charge of our village. Once a year he stops by every house to assure us of his total cooperation and he urges us to contact the police about anything suspicious. He always reminds us that we can do it anonymously, twenty-four hours a day. In small towns, the police have to rely on squealing and they know it. The mayor announced that the Symposium activities for the day were cancelled and he asked everyone to stay at home that afternoon so the police could question us. The mayor was talking with his hands, he always gets carried away.

It was a windy day and Officer Girard was having trouble with his hairdo. He was holding his hair back with his hands and the big diamond rings on his fingers were sparkling in the sun. Everyone in town made fun of his rings. Officer Girard added that he was sure he could count on the total cooperation of all the inhabitants. I told Léon he always repeated the same thing. Both men went back inside and people stayed in the parking lot, talking. The birdwatchers stood off to one side, talking among themselves. A lot of them had known Roger Lefebvre for years and they were in a state of shock.

I stayed with Léon for a long time. He decided not to open the grocery store until one in the afternoon. He stuck a sign on the door. We sat and talked on his back porch and his wife brought us some coffee. He poured two big spoonfuls of cognac into each cup. He asked me some questions. I told him how I'd driven out to Roger Lefebvre's place with Nancy and how we'd found him lying beside his van. The guy was lying on his stomach so we couldn't see where he'd been shot. Léon told me that at six o'clock the mayor was already driving around in his white Buick and he'd stopped to talk to him. Everyone in town knows that Léon gets up at five. The mayor told him that Lefebvre had been shot straight in the heart with a hunting rifle and that the police were combing the area around the cabin to find the weapon. That's when I first had my doubts. It was vague, a kind of uneasiness. I went home to have lunch and waited for the police. I was sure they'd be back to question me again.

They showed up around three. Two young officers, a guy and a girl. They shook my hand and introduced themselves. You could tell they'd just got out of the police academy, they had good manners. Nothing like Girard who always looked down on us. I made a joke about him and they laughed a bit. The girl said Officer Girard was a fine man but he had an old-fashioned idea of a policeman's role. Things had changed.

We sat down at the table and the girl asked me for a glass of water. She emptied it in one shot. They asked me the same questions as the day before. When had I seen Mr. Lefebvre for the last time? Did he have any known enemies in the village? The young guy checked his notes and asked me, "I believe Nancy is your sister?" That made me uneasy. I said yes and he asked me if I thought she was Mr. Lefebvre's mistress. That caught me off guard. When I saw her doubled up in pain in my truck, I realized that there'd been something between her and Roger Lefebvre. I'm sure they noticed that I hesitated. I told them I knew there'd been a rumour around town, but I didn't think so, and that I was convinced that my brother-in-law was incapable of shooting anyone; he didn't even go hunting. They answered that he wasn't the one who had killed Mr. Lefebvre. He hadn't left the community centre all day and at least ten people could testify to that. I mentioned that the village had been full of strangers and that nobody knew anything about Roger Lefebvre's past. Maybe they'd do better to investigate that angle. They said they were already doing that, they had the addresses of all the Symposium participants and that would facilitate matters. On her way out, the girl told me I had a beautiful yard. I commented that it was even nicer at the end of June when the yellow rose garden was in bloom.

Afterwards, I took my truck and drove around aimlessly. I couldn't stay put. I saw the mayor pacing up and down the main street. I'm sure he was in no hurry to see the name of our village associated with a murder on the front page of all the newspapers the following day. I couldn't stop thinking about Nancy. I could still see her, white as a ghost, bracing herself on the trees. I didn't have the strength to stop by her house. And then I remembered Léon and the business about the hunting rifle.

I drove out to the hunting camp and headed straight for the garage where I keep all the rifles. I opened the first case, they were all there. In the second one, a brand new 30-06 I'd bought the previous fall was missing. I remained calm. I closed the case, put the padlock back on and hid the keys in their usual place. I went over to the employees' cabin and put on some water to make myself a cup of tea. I knew that Steeve had killed Roger Lefebvre. I plugged in the radio to listen to the news. At one point, I lay down on the couch and fell asleep fully dressed. A crow's call woke me up. It was already daylight. I was starving. I went home to eat breakfast and take a shower. I was still as calm as ever.

On Monday morning I arrived at Léon's the same time as the guy delivering the newspapers. There were lots of people waiting for him. He got out of his truck and yelled, "You all made the headlines today! Looks like the guy was a good shot."

I picked up the newspaper. The only thing that interested me was the gun. It said, *The victim was killed with a 30-06 rifle, the kind used for moose hunting*. I'd already gotten used to the idea. I read on, *Lefebvre had no criminal record and the weapon has not yet been found. The police have no suspects. The village was hosting, for the third year in a row, the annual Birdwatchers Symposium. Roger Lefebvre had been an amateur ornithologist for years and had earned a reputation in the field ...* There was a picture of the village church on the front page, it was one of the photos from the tourist's guide. The headline read *Fatal Symposium*. That was it. At one point, Léon read out loud, *The police are totally in the dark*. He joked that maybe Girard's big rings could light the way. Everyone laughed. I lingered for a while on the porch of the grocery store. People believed they'd never find the murderer. The village was full of strangers, anyone could have followed him home and waited till he came out to his van.

Hearing that reassured me, I figured I was the only one who knew. I bought a case of beer from Léon. He was surprised. I usually pick up two or three cans on my way home Friday evenings and I've got enough for the weekend. It's been years since I got drunk. I went out to the camp and locked the gate behind me. I set myself up in the little cabin and waited. I was sure that Steeve would show up. Around three, I heard his ATV. He came right to me. He walked in, helped himself to a beer and sat down facing me. The kid hadn't been the same since last winter. He'd aged all of a sudden. His eyes were sunken in his puffy face. He went around wearing a plaid woollen shirt he couldn't button up anymore. He was a mess, he seemed lost. I spoke first.

"I know about old man Lefebvre."

"I figured you did."

"The gun?"

"They'll never find it."

"Why'd you do that, Steeve?"

"Because she would've left."

"Your mother?"

"Yes."

"You're sick."

"I'm not the one who's sick, it's all of you. Léon's wife left and he went on like nothing happened. Yours, too. What did you do? Nothing. You all go on like nothing's wrong. I decided to stand up for us."

"Are you sure she wanted to leave?"

"Sure. I heard her tell my father. He didn't even get mad. He went back to the shed to whittle his ducks."

"What are you going to do?"

"I'm going to Quebec City, to work in the corner store."

"When?"

"Next week. Uncle Gaétan is glad, he's been asking me for ages. How about you?"

"Nothing. I'll wait. It'll all blow over."

We drank a few beers without saying a word, like when we come back from hunting. I saw him again two or three times at Léon's and that was it. My sister told me he was glad to be working in Quebec City and that he had a girlfriend. She'd even convinced him to go back to school. I was happy for him.

The police searched the village and the surrounding area for part of the summer. By fall, we saw a lot less of them. Then came the hunting season and that kept me busy for three months. After that, it was winter. When the first big snowstorm arrived, I thought, peace, at last.

For sure, I thought about it a lot at first. Then it was like with my wife, I forgot and life went back to normal. They sold Roger Lefebvre's cabin to an actress from Montreal who's hardly ever there.

* * *

For two years in a row, we had strange winters. Very mild, too mild, according to the biologist, and with very little snow. The moose didn't even go back into the woods; you could see them everywhere around the lakes and along the roads. I'd never seen anything like it in my life. During the summer, we had a terrible drought. I had to sleep out at the camp because the risk of fire was so high.

In May of the second year, my friend the biologist came to visit the heron colony as usual. But this time he came with a young woman. It was really hot for that time of year and I dozed off while I was waiting for them.

When I woke up, they were just a few feet from my truck and the girl was holding a 30-06 covered in droppings. It was the rifle Steeve had used to shoot old man Lefebvre. She'd found it at the bottom of a dried up pond, bending over to gather the shells of eggs that had fallen from the nests. We headed back in silence. I didn't dare look them in the eye. When he left, the old guy told me he'd drop the rifle off at the police station in the neighbouring town. He added, "I know how long they've been looking for it."

I went back to the camp, for no reason, just to wait.

Élisabeth Lied

Woman is weak, and in marrying she ought to make an entire sacrifice of her will to the man who, in return, should lay his selfishness at her feet.

—Honoré de Balzac, *Letters of Two Brides* *

* Translated by R. S. Scott.

I've known Élisabeth for five years. The first summer we spent in our country house, she arrived with a jar of sweet pickles she'd made herself. I tasted them and spit out the mouthful. It was disgusting. Later she asked me about her pickles and I told her they were very good, crisp and well-seasoned. The best homemade pickles I'd ever tasted. I don't know why I insisted, especially since the jar was buried in a garbage bag. For a while, I kept worrying that Élisabeth would find the jar while walking down the road near the dump. That was pure fantasy on my part, since Élisabeth never goes anywhere without her car, but I couldn't help myself. I can't count the number of presents from Élisabeth that have ended up in the garbage since then. Her cooking is inedible. And whenever she asked me, I'd lie with the same enthusiasm. At one point, it simply became too embarrassing. That's when I got the idea of making up a blood test that had revealed a high blood sugar level after my husband's last check-up. I told Élisabeth that he and I had agreed to give up all refined sugar to avoid the risk of diabetes. I thought that would save us from all her cakes and cookies and puddings filled with chemical jelly, their colours as repulsive as their taste. But it wasn't enough to dissuade her. She told me there was no reason why I should have to give up sweets. When I went to visit her, I was often treated to one of her frozen cookies that she nukes in her microwave. She serves them on a fancy plate on the counter strewn with bills from the farm. She would watch me taste her latest baking feat as she awaited my verdict. One time the cookie was filled with mint jelly and strawberry jam. I had to close my eyes and concentrate on not feeling sick to my stomach. It was like swallowing half a tube of toothpaste. I can't imagine how she managed to reproduce the taste of Colgate's spearmint, unadulterated. The soft, gooey texture of the cookie only reinforced this sensation.

Whenever Élisabeth came to visit us, my husband would take refuge in some urgent work to be done, a report to be delivered to his research associate the following day, and he'd lock himself up in his study. Most of the time, I'd find him wearing his earphones, playing one of his favourite video games. We had several talks about this. He thought Élisabeth was dishonest and petty and he didn't approve of my being so friendly with her. He spent his days in the country cooped up in his study writing or preparing his courses. He's such a daydreamer I doubt that he could remember the name of our closest neighbours. He doesn't have anything to do with anyone, and doesn't wish to. He is there to work. The only thing that interests him is his current project. He says that no matter what we do, our relations with people from the village will never be one of equals, and that they only put up with us because we, and the other owners of country houses, are an important source of income. In his opinion, the relationship is economic and all the rest is just a sinister masquerade. I tell him he has a nineteenth-century view of the world, and he retorts that the village is still back in the nineteenth century, so he is more in tune with it than I am.

At first, I was convinced that my husband was wrong about Élisabeth. I felt he didn't understand the way she behaved. I kept telling him that Élisabeth truly believed what she said. She lived in a *Reader's Digest* world, where the bad guys were clearly identified and made the front page of the tabloids. I couldn't convince him. He was sure that Élisabeth was cultivating a friendship with me only because of my social status and that it helped preserve her prestige in the village. She and her husband owned one of the last big farms in the region, and their daughters had gone to university. Furthermore, why were all her friends from outside the village? His sharp criticism of Élisabeth surprised me more than it bothered me. He rarely expressed an opinion about other people and he had left all our social obligations up to me ages ago. It was the first time he'd made such a radical comment about one of my friends. I'd never heard him use the word *petty*.

I don't know why, but I cared about my relationship with Élisabeth. I did recognize that my husband was right about one thing: all her friends were from outside the village. But I attributed that to coincidence, not to a deliberate choice on her part. And I have to admit, throughout our friendship, I often lied to her. I thought she was too vulnerable to deal with reality as I saw it. In a way, I was condescending.

Élisabeth was very proud of her friendships with summer residents, and she regularly told me about their lives and their problems even if I had no connection with them.

Occasionally I felt that she took great pleasure in announcing all the catastrophes, real or imagined, that befell them. But what she enjoyed most was telling me about their health problems: cancer, heart attacks, degenerative diseases that kept striking them or members of their family. As if divine justice did not spare the rich who were not forced to spend their lives on a farm and who could go shopping every day, something Élisabeth admitted was her dream.

She felt contempt for farmers and particularly for her husband, even though he owned the most prosperous dairy farm in the area. Her contempt for everything about farm life and especially the smell of milk her husband carried with him dismayed me. It was as if she felt shame, a kind of archaic shame associated with the peasant condition. In the cellar of their old farmhouse, she'd made him build a true decontamination chamber, worthy of a quarantine camp. First there was a dressing room where he could undress, then a little room with a shower and finally another room with the clothes he was only allowed to wear in the house. It was the first thing she showed me, although she lives in a beautifully preserved two-hundred-year-old farmhouse full of pine furniture hand-made by her husband's great-grandfather. She often said to me, "It doesn't smell in here, not like the other farmhouses." For her, that was a huge victory. She finds any cheese worthy of that name disgusting and can't stand the taste of yogurt. She buys commercial milk for coffee only and bright-orange Kraft cheese slices individually wrapped in plastic to garnish their hamburgers.

Her husband seems to put up with her demands. In the summertime, he often chooses not to come back into the house before evening, so as not to waste his time going through the whole decontamination procedure. They have their noon meal on the back porch. She serves him a fricassee of vegetables and unidentified meat that's been stewing since six in the morning in an electric clay cooker. She adds the potatoes and carrots around eleven in the morning. Apparently it's always the same menu. I often watched Élisabeth add the vegetables. She looks up at the clock, sighs and reaches under the sink. She takes out an old pot full of limp carrots and potatoes beginning to sprout. She sighs as she peels them. This is a real performance: all her self-denial, her abnegation and her devotion are apparent in the way she executes this simple daily chore. She was sacrificing herself, and her sacrifice was great. I was a witness.

At one point, I stopped mentioning her to my husband. I didn't tell him about our conversations. I didn't want to admit that my friendship with Élisabeth was a welcome change of pace. I was about to turn fifty, I was exhausted by the constant battle my work represented, and I found it reassuring to spend time with Élisabeth whose life was regulated like clockwork. I envied her set beliefs. For the first time in a long time, I felt safe.

I told Élisabeth everything: my joys, my disappointments, my professional problems, my thoughts about life in the village. Élisabeth always listened quietly and reassured me. Her vocabulary came straight from the women's shows she watched all day on the little TV on her kitchen counter, and she had adopted the same soothing, psychological jargon that turns women's brains to marshmallow. I let myself surrender to her silly sentimentalism and I stopped resisting. There was something reassuring about Élisabeth's notion of willing sacrifice, it had a soothing effect on me.

All I knew about Élisabeth was what she told me. She'd met her husband when she was twenty-seven and at the time, people were already calling her "the old nurse." She was working at the hospital in the closest city and they'd met at a dance. She didn't hesitate long, even though the prospect of spending her life on a farm was not what she'd dreamed of. He had spent a few months in Montreal, and just when he found a job delivering heating oil, his father had a stroke, and he came back. Élisabeth had added, between gritted teeth, "He never could say no to them." So she had spent the first years of her marriage with a mother-in-law on her back and a helpless father-in-law, stuck in a wheelchair and needing care. Élisabeth always talks about this period with bitterness in her voice.

She has two daughters. They live in distant cities and show no interest in this godforsaken village and the dairy farm. In fact, she has passed on to them her dislike for animals and all dairy products, a dislike that often translates into the contemptuous comments they make about their father's profession.

My friendship with her was important to me. I realized just how important when she betrayed me. I thought I had found a kind of sisterhood with her, but I later realized that the apparent solidarity was false, like the illusion of solidarity that lasts for the hour of a daytime talk show. Élisabeth's feelings were as deep as the sentimental programs she watched.

The truth was that Élisabeth was trapped in the country and she'd been isolated from the rest of the world for too long. In the summer, the time she spent with strangers was like a game. It was of no consequence to her, at the very most, a break in the routine of her life. She knew she was condemned to spend her existence with this silent man whose smell made her sick. Over the years, she'd become a troubled woman, a misfit incapable of feeling any real emotion or having a truly personal opinion. She always waited for the other person to express an opinion on a subject, so she could quickly agree. She glommed onto strangers because they were so impressed by her house and her antiques, all things people in the country take for granted or despise. She'd become obsessive about decorating her house. There was no life in Élisabeth's house, she lived in a museum where antique dolls with china heads and christening gowns slept on her daughters' beds. There was even one doll, an infant version, lying in an old wicker basket at the foot of her bed. A disturbing thought, when I imagined this couple approaching their sixties going to bed every night at the bedside of a newborn child with a painted face. I finally understood that Élisabeth's life was held together by sentimentality and hatred. A strange blend I found fascinating.

For several years, I only spent time with Élisabeth during the two summer months. My husband and I would go back to Montreal at the end of August to prepare for the fall session. I'd call her occasionally over the winter. Then, last year, I finally had a sabbatical. I stayed in the country, intending to complete a research report that was long overdue. It was the first time in a long time that I'd been separated from my husband and I felt lonely. I saw Élisabeth almost every morning. In the afternoon, instead of working on my book, I'd lose myself in a novel, surfacing around four, slightly depressed and glad that cocktail hour was approaching. Then I'd start cooking an unnecessarily complicated meal, too complicated at least for a person living alone, and by the time I sat down to dinner I'd already drunk half a bottle of wine and a glass of scotch. I'd go to bed early and slightly drunk. I told my husband my work was going well, when in truth I hadn't even looked at my research files. I was spending no time at my desk.

After a few weeks of this idleness, I became interested in what was going on in the village, in the comings and goings of my neighbours, especially since, after the lull at the end of the vacation months, life seemed to be picking up. People were preparing their houses for the hunters' arrival. It was the first time I'd lived in our house during the hunting season and I'd never seen the village so lively.

One morning, when I went to see Élisabeth, I found her cleaning the three rooms where her in-laws had lived, the "annex" as she called it. She kept it for when her daughters came to visit. That's what she'd told me. She greeted me, saying she'd been working there since six in the morning, that her husband had gone to fetch the guide and her first hunters were due to arrive at ten on Saturday morning. Everything had to be ready. She obviously had forgotten what she'd told me before. She'd always claimed that contrary to other women in the village, she never offered accommodation to hunters. They were often drunk and dirtied the houses with their mud-caked clothes. On top of that, they were loud and ill-mannered. She showed me the mountain of cookies she'd prepared and her husband's home-baked bread. I remarked that it was a lot of work, to which she replied, with her usual sense of sacrifice, that a person had to earn a living. I thought she had lied to me because she was ashamed of lodging hunters, it was like admitting they needed money.

I hardly saw her at all during the entire hunting season. The two or three times I stopped by her husband greeted my coolly, as if to say that Élisabeth had better things to do than waste her time with me who didn't need to work. So I finally began to enter the results of my research on my computer. It wasn't much but it was a start. And I tried to limit my alcohol consumption. I was beginning to think that solitude didn't suit me and that it might be better for me to go back to Montreal. I missed the comfort of my apartment and, over the years, I'd become dependent upon my husband. I missed his quiet presence and his scathing sense of humour. But I decided to stay.

I could hardly recognize the peaceful village where we spent our summers. There was a kind of tension bubbling beneath the surface everywhere, at the grocery store, the post office. Everyone talked in a tone of voice an octave higher than usual. The traffic began at five in the morning and ended in the late afternoon with the procession of the few lucky hunters. They cruised down the main street, with the moose rack displayed on the hood of their trucks. They drove with three or four of them crowded into a cab that could only hold two, passing each other cans of beer and tossing the empties into the back of the truck. That lasted for a few days and then it was all over.

The hunting season was finished. Once again the village was silent and the inhabitants less anxious. I sent an email telling my husband that everything was back to normal and that people had probably been unsettled by the presence of death everywhere. He replied that they had been thrilled by all the money pouring out of the hunters' pockets.

One morning, when I was dividing my perennials, Élisabeth's husband drove by. He was wearing his black leather coat and I thought he must be on his way to the city. A bit later, I went to bring her some bulbs. She wasn't in the house. Her neighbour's tractor was parked outside the stable. As I headed in that direction, I could hear laughter and a noise I couldn't identify. I went up to the door that was wide open. Élisabeth was handing kittens to the neighbour who was throwing them with all his might against the concrete wall in front of him. You could hear the creatures' bones break. Then they'd fall on the ground, leaving bloodstains on the wall. Élisabeth noticed me. She came towards me smiling, saying thank heavens she had André to help her disinfect the stable since her husband was incapable of killing a fly. Every fall they had the same problem, the barn was invaded by cats. Someone had to act. I withdrew, I didn't want to see the bodies lying on the ground. She was wearing rubber gloves and holding a garbage bag. She smelled of bleach. I gave her the gladiola bulbs she'd asked for and I left almost immediately, claiming I was expecting an important call. It wasn't true. I needed to escape.

For days afterwards, I didn't leave my computer. I didn't even take my usual walks. It was as if writing that report became a question of life or death. Sometimes, I remembered the sound of bones shattering against the concrete and the smell of bleach. I finally managed to convince myself that I was too sensitive, and one way or another, you couldn't allow cats to breed out of control. I had an urban way of looking at things and that's why I was shocked.

One morning, very early, Élisabeth knocked at my door in tears. She was still wearing her barn clothes. She insisted upon taking her boots off on the porch. She stood on my rug, her fists clenched, unable to speak. She finally managed to mutter, "Sorry about the smell."

I shrugged and asked, "What's wrong?"

"What's wrong is what's always wrong, we can't go away."

"You won't be going to visit your daughter?"

She was supposed to go to Halifax at the end of the month.

"No, he can't find anyone to take care of the farm."

"You could go on your own."

"Marius won't let me. It costs too much by plane and he doesn't like staying on the farm without me."

"There must be some solution."

"No is no. You don't know him."

I took her by the arm and sat her down. She was still crying. I could feel her anger. I made some coffee and I don't know what came over me, but I invited her to come to Montreal with me. I'd finished my report and wanted to submit my first draft to one of my colleagues. We could stay for three or four days. She could go shopping while I tended to my affairs. She told me she'd think about it. I knew she would have to ask permission. She calmed down.

Élisabeth was disappointed. She'd been looking forward to that trip for a long time. She'd mentioned it to me several times. It would be her first visit to another province. Her daughter had been living there for two years and she'd never seen her house, except in pictures. The damn farm was spoiling everything.

She talked about the arrival of winter. It made her very anxious. She didn't know how she'd managed to put up with it for so many years. She claimed I could never understand. She was convinced that winter there was harsher than anywhere else and very few people could take it. In her mind, Montreal was in the South.

The following day she called to say that she might stay with her sister-in-law in Boucherville. They hadn't seen each other for a long time and they got along well. I'd be free to tend to my business and could pick her up on the way back. To be honest, I was relieved. I didn't know how to announce my unexpected visit with Élisabeth to my husband. We left two days later shortly before dawn. I prefer to drive very early in the morning. The weather was misty and it was drizzling. I'd checked the on-line weather report three times to make sure it wasn't going to turn to freezing rain.

We must have been driving for half an hour when I noticed a big pickup ahead of me, completing some strange manoeuvre. It was still dark and it was hard to see what was happening, but I saw a man at the edge of the woods throw something into the back of the truck. Then he ran to the cab and they took off in a flash. I had the feeling they fled when they saw my car. I stopped at the spot where I'd seen them. Walking along the roadside, I could feel something sticky underfoot. It was blood. I went over to the ditch and I could see the moose still steaming. The animal had been trapped and the poachers had just cut it in two with a chainsaw and taken the hindquarters. Élisabeth was standing beside me. I moved away and vomited the fruit and the yogurt I'd eaten before leaving.

We got back into the car and drove to the next village. I couldn't find a phone. Everything was closed. It was still too early. I had to wait till we reached the highway. I had a sour taste in my mouth. I exited at the first service station. I gargled in the sink in the washroom. I called my husband. I was so furious I needed to hear his voice. The first time, the answering machine kicked in. I called back and waited for the beep. I shouted his name. He picked up the phone. I told him the whole story: that I was still on the road, that I'd vomited, that I thought they had cut up the animal while it was still alive. He told me to call S.O.S. Poaching, that the operator would give me the number. He also told me to calm down and he said he loved me. I started to cry.

I waited a bit, then I called. A woman's sleepy voice told me I could remain anonymous. I gave her my name, address and telephone number. I described where the animal was. She told me an officer would go to the site immediately. I told her that I was on my way to Montreal when I saw a big dark-coloured pickup. No, I couldn't tell her the license plate number or the colour. It was too dark. I hung up.

Élisabeth was waiting for me in the car. She was drinking

a cup of coffee from a vending machine. It smelled like burnt cardboard. She offered me some. I refused. She told me not to be so upset, that it happened all the time and there wasn't much to be done about it. I could sense that she thought I was exaggerating, but she nodded at my comments. Around noon, we stopped at a McDonald's. I wasn't hungry, so I had a cup of stale orange pekoe and studied the map so I wouldn't get lost in Boucherville. I dropped Élisabeth off at her sister-in-law's house and went straight home. It must have been around two and my husband wasn't back from work. I took a bath in my old-fashioned bathtub and I noticed that everything smelled of lemon oil. The cleaning woman must have come recently. I raided the fridge and found some leftover taboulé and some bruschetta. In the cupboard there were some crackers and the bottles of white wine we keep in reserve. I opened a bottle and chilled my glass with an ice cube. I went into my office and before sorting through the pile of mail from the previous two months, I called S.O.S. Poaching. It wasn't the same person. Yes, the officer had gone to the site, he had found the remains of the animal and opened an investigation. I gave my telephone number and address in the country, which I'd neglected to give the first time.

My husband came home with mussels, fresh tuna and a bottle of Sancerre. He laughed and said he had a soul to heal. I told him about the village, about the hunting season, the work I'd done on the flowerbeds. I didn't mention the episode with the kittens. I don't know why, but sitting there with him in our dining room, it made me feel ashamed.

I walked around the city for three days. It was early

November but the weather was unseasonably mild. I met my colleague in a café on Laurier Street. Elegant women, wrapped in cashmere shawls, were hurrying by the restaurants and boutiques. I even found this bourgeois display pleasant. I stopped thinking about the moose. In my mind, the case was closed. I'd done the right thing.

Élisabeth was waiting for me on the front steps of her sister-in-law's house. She'd been to the hairdresser and was featuring red streaks in her already dyed auburn hair. The effect was dubious, but I said it looked pretty. She'd been shopping for three days in a row, her sister-in-law knew all the best places. She was surrounded by shopping bags. Before we left, she absolutely had to show me something. The object was inside. I went in with her and said hello to a tall boy who was standing at the kitchen counter making toast. Élisabeth said, "This is Luc." Then she started to painstakingly unwrap a package. It was a china doll, in seventeenth-century dress, posing in a minuet position. It must have been a foot high. She thought she'd put it on the piano, what did I think? It had cost a hundred dollars; a woman deserves to splurge once in a while. I touched the doll with my fingertips. The china was cold. It was ghastly. I couldn't help but imagine my husband's reaction, I don't know why, but he loathes dolls. I said, "It's beautiful." Then I helped her wrap it up again. She said goodbye to the teenage boy.

We loaded the car and we left. On the road, Élisabeth was very talkative. She told me about her visit, about all the presents she had bought. She had something for me, but she wanted to show it to her husband first and have him sign the card. Her sister-in-law had been wonderful with her, they'd eaten out in a restaurant almost every evening. She listed off the places she'd been. I didn't know any of them, much to her surprise. I explained that Boucherville was quite a ways from my house and that I always tended to go to the same places. She commented that I seemed unusually quiet and I said I didn't talk much when I drove, I needed to concentrate.

The weather was beautiful, bright and sunny. It felt like early autumn. We drove through the village where we'd looked for a phone. I mentioned the animal again. Then Élisabeth made a comment that surprised me.

"Marius said you shouldn't have called."

"Why?"

"Because they won't do anything and it could be bad for the owners of the hunting camps if game wardens started hanging out in the village."

I was a bit annoyed and answered, "To my knowledge, the hunting season was over."

"Yes, but Marius thinks you shouldn't have done it anyway. He says it's none of our business."

I was really mad.

"What about you, Élisabeth, what do you think?"

"I think you let your conscience be your guide, that's what matters."

She'd just answered with one of her virtuous comments that no one could dispute. Then she changed the subject. She kept repeating that this trip had done her a world of good and would give her the strength to get through the winter. She asked me how long I expected to stay. I said we were thinking of spending the holidays in the country. It was something we'd wanted to do for a long time.

Her husband was waiting for us to arrive. We unloaded the car. I found him a bit distant. He'd never been particularly friendly to me and this time I thought he held me responsible for Élisabeth's expensive outing. People say he's stingy. I didn't let it bother me. I went to the grocery store to buy some bottled water, and again, I found the grocer a bit short. He had always been very nice to me. It made me feel uncomfortable and I promised myself that if it happened again, I'd ask for an explanation. My husband and I went out of our way to patronize his store during our summer vacation to support the village economy. I wouldn't hesitate. I was struggling not to hear my husband's voice saying, "An economic relationship, purely economic."

I waited for my colleague's comments and I resumed work at a disciplined pace. It was finished within a matter of days. At last I had a final draft of my report. I wanted to take advantage of the time remaining until Christmas to rest and to read. I took long walks in the afternoon and went to bed early. After a week had gone by, I realized that I hadn't seen Élisabeth and she hadn't called me either.

One morning a young woman in a beige uniform knocked on my door. She was a game warden. She began by saying she wished everyone had my sense of civic responsibility and that the investigation was still underway. They had their suspicions but my description of the truck was too vague and the poachers had had time to remove any clues. She was in the vicinity and simply wanted to thank me. A complaint always made them lie low for a while. I offered her a cup of coffee. She was the first person I'd seen in a week. She followed me into the kitchen and went into rapture over my espresso machine. She loved coffee, this was going to be her next purchase. I told her where I'd bought it on Dante Street in Montreal. I said I was sure they would accept a telephone order. She wrote down the name of the store. She commented, slightly surprised, "They sell hunting rifles, too. They're specialists." I said yes. I'd forgotten that. She often saw their name on documents. We sat down at the table. She asked me if there was anything new. I said no. Then I thought of my conversation with Élisabeth. I told her I was with my neighbour when we found the animal. She consulted her papers and saw no mention of that. I didn't know why I hadn't told them, I must have been too upset and nobody asked the question. And then, remembering Élisabeth's comments, I had a kind of revelation. I was sure she knew who the poachers were, perhaps she had even recognized the truck. I told the warden everything. She said Élisabeth would never talk. No one in the village ever talked, except anonymously to denounce a rival hunting camp, and then only to harm them or to take revenge. I saw her head towards the farm.

Around one o'clock, there was a knock at my door again. It was Élisabeth's husband. He had never set foot in my house. He never went out anywhere in the village. He was nervous, he's not a man who's used to talking. I asked him to come in. He remained in the doorway, without closing the door. He told me he'd spent his whole life in the village, and neither he nor his family had ever had trouble with anyone and it wasn't going to start now. People had always sorted things out without involving the police. He wanted me to know that Élisabeth hadn't seen anything on the road because she was dozing and, besides, she was short-sighted. That's what she told the game warden. He'd been living here for fifty years and he hoped this would be the first and the last time a game warden ever showed up at his door. He raised his voice. Was that clear? Furthermore, he and a lot of other people had had just about enough of the strangers in the village. He slammed the door and left.

I started to cry. I didn't want to admit it, but he had really frightened me. It wasn't only his words, it was the hatred inside him that scared me. That hatred had hit me hard and I was shaken. I wandered around the house most of the afternoon. Around four o'clock, I went for a walk. I vaguely hoped I'd run into Élisabeth who usually came back from her rounds in the village around that time. She liked to take her car and drive up and down the main street at the end of the afternoon. Then she'd go home and get ready to help her husband with the evening milking. I didn't run into her. I didn't dare walk by her house. For days after that, I kept getting up in the night to make sure my doors were locked. When I went back to the grocery store, I was treated to the same cool reception and this time, I reacted. I asked what the problem was. The grocer is a nervous, moody man. He replied that because of that business last week, the police and the game wardens would be snooping around for weeks to come. I asked him how that would affect him and he couldn't answer. I said it wasn't normal to saw animals in half while they were still alive and that I wasn't about to stand by and say nothing. His wife arrived, probably alerted by the sound of our voices, and she, who never says a word, dared take my side. She had always found that behaviour unacceptable. He calmed down and admitted that he was worried it would affect the hunting camps. I suggested that his survival depended more on people like me who spent long periods in the village than on a few hunters who only came for a few days. His wife agreed again. I asked him to prepare my bill when he had time, because I thought I'd be returning to Montreal soon. When I went back, he was his usual courteous self, a bit too courteous maybe.

When I finally saw Élisabeth again, I was picking bulrushes along the side of the road. I didn't recognize her at first. She drove by very fast in a little red car. I knew that she'd wanted a new car for a long time. I raised my hand to wave to her and she acted as if she didn't see me. She had traded me for a new car.

Beautiful Like Jeanne Moreau

"THE WEATHER'S SO NICE, if it keeps up like this, we'll be able to do the Virgin Mary. We're late this year."

I gave Martine a startled look. It took me a few seconds to realize that she was talking about the statue at the entrance to the village. Of course, I knew that she and her Uncle Omer were the ones who maintained it. In early June, as soon as the weather turns warm, Martine washes the Virgin with warm, soapy water and Omer touches up her makeup with a bit of acrylic paint. The village has the most made-up statue in the province and the first time I saw it, it reminded me of those gaudy Mexican Virgins.

"Yes, the weather's great. After the past few chilly days, it's hard to believe that summer is finally here. Would you like another margarita?"

"No, I don't have time. Raynald is coming to pick me up for the film. They're shooting some scenes at the hunting camp. I have to open the gates for them."

"When will it come out?"

"Maybe next year, they're not sure."

We talked a bit about the film that was supposed to help promote the region and the village, and that, as I would later realize, turned out to be a barely disguised advertisement for the hunting camp on the mountain. The owners had decided to keep it open in the summertime, by catering to city people looking for the wilderness experience. The film was Raynald's idea. I wondered what he would get out of it. He made sure there was something for him in everything he did.

Martine began to defend Raynald. It was the same old tune: Raynald was getting publicity for the village. Raynald had a successful career in Montreal. Raynald was friends with lots of well-known artists. This argument always drove me mad. I cut her off. I pointed out a green car headed towards her house, no, it wasn't Raynald's. We watched it turn around in her driveway. She added, in her resigned tone of voice that never fails to rile me, "There'll be more and more strangers around, it's that time of the year." She left for home. She was wearing a pale blue dress, she'd copied the design from the *Vogue* catalogue at the village dry goods store. The dress was perfectly cut and fit her like a glove. She seemed totally unaware of her incredible beauty. She looked like Jeanne Moreau in *Jules et Jim*. I never told her so, convinced that she wouldn't have known who I was talking about. She was a magnificent woman, intelligent, but, as my husband said, "a fallow field." She hadn't been able to finish high school.

Martine lives in the last house on our range line. From there on, the road is no more than a little track for tractors leading to the mountain. It's unfit for cars. Everyone turns around in her driveway. That happens a lot in the summer. At night, the noise wakes up her husband. It prevents him from sleeping. She's always saying how nervous he is.

Martine is probably around thirty-eight. She was adopted by a family in the village but the gossips say her real mother still lives here. Martine had admitted that to me long before I heard it from anyone else. It was the day of the tornado, barely a month after we'd bought our house. Once the wind died down, she came to visit me. She knew I was alone and wanted to see if our house had been damaged. The window in the front door was the only thing broken. She would send her Uncle Omer to repair it. I offered her a cup of tea, she hesitated before accepting. She sat very straight at the end of the table. We chatted for a while, a heavy rain began to fall and out of the blue, she told me, point-blank, for no reason, that she'd been adopted, and that people had decided to let her know that her real parents were still in the village. What would I do in her place? I had just arrived and I couldn't imagine how a person could live for years knowing something like that and carrying on as if she were unaware. Since then, I have discovered, at my expense, that lying is the golden rule in the village. Everyone knows everything and everyone pretends to know nothing. I replied that in my opinion she should settle the matter before her real parents disappeared. After that, she left and for over a year I only ran into her by chance at the post office or the grocery store. It was as if she had never told me a thing. She was distant and polite. It was a long time before she came back to visit me. Obviously, someone in the village finally told us the story and revealed the identity of her real parents. She has never broached the subject again. Now she often stops by in the summer, at the end of the day, and spends an hour or two with me. I make us margaritas. She loves the effect of tequila.

I went back into the house to serve myself another drink

and to drag my husband out of his study. I couldn't help but complain about Raynald. Raynald personified all the unbearable traits of the country poet. He was full of himself and flaunted his superiority all around town. He was an example of the worst results of certain cultural policies. Year in and year out, he received one grant after another to write what I called *Tales of Our Pioneer Past*—books of stories, usually badly written, in which he claimed to record the legacy of a people. He was a very bad writer, but he had figured out how the system worked. He had mastered the use of government jargon in the field of culture, especially in the area of regional cultural activities. Any criticism of him would have been attributed to Montreal snobbism which, as everyone knows, consists of scorn for everything done outside of the metropolitan area. He was beyond reproach. Every time we met him, and it was always at the restaurant in the neighbouring village, the only restaurant worthy of this name in a fifty-kilometre radius, he'd always come to chat with us and flatter me about my work. He'd always read the latest article I'd published. After all, wasn't he an ethnologist in his own right? And he never failed to make fun of the restaurant in our village. I was careful not to agree with him. He would have been all too happy to go around repeating it everywhere. I'd answer vaguely that the menu was "traditional." But what made me really furious was the way he manipulated the village by promoting the most preposterous projects. They saw him as a saviour and there was nothing to be said or done. I often repeated to my husband that he had only one talent, but it was considerable.

When he spoke, I don't know how he managed it, but he always sounded as if he was speaking the truth. He talked in a low voice, and frequently paused. He seemed to be choosing each and every word.

He always waited till early September to promote his projects. Once the summer residents had left, the coast was clear. No one ever dared question his ideas. They were all too terrified by the prospect of the village possibly being closed down. In my opinion, the worst had already happened. The village had died a long time ago, it had slowly become a holiday town, a country retreat for rich professional people from the city looking for peace and quiet.

On at least two occasions, his undertakings had been disastrous. He'd had the brilliant idea of creating a summer theatre where amateur actors from the village and so-called professionals (he'd hired second-rate sitcom actors) would perform a play based on the historical founding of the village. It was such a dismal failure, they had to cancel the performances after the first week. Obviously, the municipality lost the several thousand dollars they'd invested in the fiasco. Another time, he'd set up greenhouses to grow vegetables during the winter; again, it was a catastrophe. The people he hired had no experience and all the seedlings had died, drowned; the employees had no idea how to control the sprinkler system. The two greenhouses still stand in the field behind the church and the wind has begun to blow holes in the plastic. Omer says they should be demolished, they're infested with field mice and garter snakes. Every time I drive by, I can't help but think of the two employees who, after their failure, had stayed holed up in their houses for days. They were ashamed. Omer told me about it. He said, "You have to realize, they boasted that they'd be supplying the village year round. And less than a month after they started, they had flooded everything. One of the young guys called me in a panic. I told him to turn off the electricity. That night, everything froze. It was a pity."

Omer has been taking care of our house since the day of the famous tornado. He also maintains many other country houses around here and in the next village over. He's a solitary man who has always lived with his sister. He is mistrustful, and his mistrust is instinctive. It took a while before he trusted me. He has let down his guard over the years. He's the only one in the village who shares my aversion for Raynald. He always says, "I'm not about to bow and scrape, just because he put my name in one of his books. My name isn't Clément."

Clément is the municipal clerk and Martine's nervous husband. According to Omer, he is Raynald's valet. He spends most of his summers in Raynald's car, accompanying him everywhere. Clément is tall and thin, like a gangly teenager with arms too long for his body. His voice is jerky. Once at a town meeting, I heard him stutter. You'd never think he was over forty. He studied accounting, and he's been the village clerk ever since. That was his goal. Martine knew she would marry him when she was a little girl. I asked her why. She was amazed by my question: "Because I knew him well, we started going out when I was twelve or thirteen. It was normal." Then she avoided my glance. She was uncomfortable. She had never questioned her choice. When I went back inside, I told my husband. I was flabbergasted. This wasn't the nineteenth century. He laughed and replied, "Aren't you the expert? That's how it is in the country." I turned my back to him, he was unfair. A true city slicker, he was amused to see his ethnologist wife mystified by her neighbours' behaviour.

In July there was a terrible heat wave, the worst the village had ever seen. No one could talk about anything else. One evening, Martine and I were sitting in the porch swing when Clément came to join us. The heat had forced him out of the house. I knew from Martine that in addition to his work for the municipality, he wrote novels. "True stories that happened in this village," she had specified. One day she brought me a copy of Clément's only published title. It had been published at the author's expense. After fifteen years of writing, he had been unable to find a publisher. The book told the story of a village pioneer and his wife who, during the Spanish flu epidemic, had lost all their children, except for one son who was miraculously spared. He had preserved their lineage. There was a preface by Saint Raynald, praising the work of Clément, who, like himself, was a guardian of remembrance. The book was so naïve, I was embarrassed for him. I had no idea what to say to him. Obviously, I lied. I bluffed my way through, talking about the importance of local history.

My husband came out to join us. Clément started searching for words. That made me uncomfortable. When he spoke to Maurice, he became even more anxious and felt the need to tackle serious subjects and use a vocabulary he didn't master. He didn't act that way with me, although I am every bit as much a professor as my husband.

I suggested we have some rosé. After two bottles, the atmosphere was more relaxed and my husband invited them to share our salad with us. They accepted. When they left, we promised we'd go to taste Clément's spaghetti with veal meatballs. He prepared it every Friday during the summer. I offered to bring the appetizer. Later, while putting away the dishes, I realized we had spent seven summers in the village and this was the first time anyone had invited us to supper.

That Friday, as promised, we went to Martine's to taste the "Friday-night spaghetti," as Clément called it. Most of the old houses in the village have been renovated inside to look like suburban bungalows. At Martine's, all the walls have been taken down and the ground floor is one open space. The dining area next to the kitchen is furnished with a white melamine dining set. A leaf had been added to the table. I was surprised, since there were only four of us.

I put my tapas on the counter and suggested that we have our before-dinner drinks and hors d'oeuvres on the back porch. My suggestion took them off guard. It wasn't something they did. I could tell by their reaction. We went outside and Clément went to bring some chairs from the front porch. Several cars came to turn around in their driveway. Every time Clément went to see who it was. When he got back, he had trouble picking up the conversation. He was worried, that was obvious, his breathing was even irregular. At one point, I got up to serve the wine. It felt like they were waiting for someone.

Finally, we went back inside. Martine cooked the pasta and we ate. She had prepared a maple sugar pie for dessert. We refused their offer of coffee.

We went outside and chatted for a long time on their porch. It was late when we headed home. Martine lent us a flashlight and we cut across the field. When we arrived, I sat down outside and spent part of the night there. It was hot and I felt as if the meatballs were hard to digest. I drank cup after cup of tisane. At dawn, I finally went to bed. I realized that it was Clément I couldn't digest. I couldn't understand his attitude, something escaped me. I nudged Maurice and he grunted a bit. I asked him if he had found Clément's behaviour strange. He told me to sleep, that Clément's behaviour was always strange. What could I say? He was right as usual.

Martine didn't come to visit for two or three days. When I ran into her on the road, she told me she was replacing someone on the film crew. She was enthusiastic, she was learning a lot about camerawork and lighting. She was a real help to them, since she knew all the prettiest views in the village. The cameraman had insisted on filming her by the river. She laughed, she hoped he wouldn't keep this footage for the film. Martine usually works at her sister's bed and breakfast during the summer. They finish making up the rooms by noon and she goes home. She spends part of the afternoon working in her garden and around four o'clock, she comes to see me. Most of the time, she talks about her sister's customers and how dirty they are. She hates to think of their houses. There's nothing to be said. I've tried to explain that they pay for their rooms and that money also covers housekeeping, that's the way it works. I realized that for her, their dirtiness went beyond the state of the room after their departure, it had more to do with being soiled, sinful. Her archaic views of the world both fascinated and annoyed me. She was all submission and resignation. For Martine, the world had a meaning and an order, that of the village. I envied her serenity.

That Wednesday or Thursday, I can't remember, she appeared at the far side of the field, wearing a low-cut red dress. She'd put up her hair because of the heat. I'd never seen her look more beautiful. I got up from my chair and went to join her. We inspected my flowers. Over the years, I had planted the bulbs she had given me and the results were beginning to show. I had grown an astilbe I was quite proud of. She laughed at my enthusiasm. For Martine, you plant a seed and flowers grow, that's all there is to it. We sat down in the swing, as usual, and she told me about the film. She'd loved the experience. She told me about the cameraman again. She said he was very calm. There had been a big fight during the shoot between Raynald and the director. That had surprised her, but the cameraman told her it happened all the time. He usually made nature films, but occasionally he accepted other contracts to pay his rent. I listened distractedly. I waited until she finished and then I couldn't help myself, I mentioned our supper together.

"Martine, you should have told us you didn't want to sit out back, I didn't mean to force you. I could see that Clément was uncomfortable."

"Don't be silly, we don't sit there often, but it doesn't matter."

"What was bothering Clément?"

"What do you mean?"

"He kept getting up every time a car came into the drive."

"Oh, that! He was just checking to see if Raynald was coming."

"Had you invited him?"

"In the summer, Clément makes his spaghetti sauce every Friday. Raynald's the one who christened it 'the Friday-night spaghetti.' Sometimes he comes, sometimes he doesn't."

"He doesn't let you know in advance?"

I'd almost shouted. Martine started.

"No, it doesn't matter, Clément makes his sauce anyway."

"So, every Friday you wait for him before eating."

"Not in the winter, just the summer."

"How do you decide when it's time to eat?"

"Around six-thirty, if he hasn't arrived, that usually means he's not coming."

Martine answered as if she were talking about the weather. I was scandalized, I'd seen how it affected Clément.

"Don't you find it makes Clément more nervous?"

"He's always nervous anyway."

"But that makes it worse, doesn't it? Perhaps it would be better for Clément if Raynald let you know in advance. He wouldn't have the anxiety of waiting."

She gave me a strange look. I realized it was the way I'd just spoken to her. I had never been so sharp or direct. I was on a roll, unable to prevent myself.

"It's unacceptable. It's the height of domination! Who does he think he is? The Messiah?"

Martine couldn't understand why I was getting so carried away. I finally calmed down and said it was none of my business. She didn't utter a word for several minutes. Then she got up and went home. I knew I shouldn't have let myself get carried away, that I shouldn't have judged the situation. I had broken the law of the village. I had tears in my eyes, I felt like a little girl who's just lost her best friend and I was ashamed.

Martine didn't come back to see me all summer. I didn't try to talk to her. In town, we simply nodded to each other. On Friday, I couldn't help it, I looked to see which cars went to her house. I saw Raynald go by sometimes, often with two or three people. My husband said Raynald was saving his money. He was right.

* * *

I waved to Omer. He was parked facing the statue. I'd been in the village for a week and I still hadn't seen him. I stopped my car beside his. He was the one who spoke first.

"You're already here? Seems like it's earlier than last year."

"Yes, I've come by myself, my husband's still working."

"Everything all right at the house?"

"Yes, no problem."

"I suppose you've heard?"

"Heard what, Omer?"

I knew him, he had something serious to announce.

"Martine left. She left like the other women. They're all leaving."

I stared at him. I knew he meant she had left Clément.

"When did she leave?"

"In the fall, just before the hunting season. One of the guys from the film came to get her one Saturday."

"How's Clément?"

"They say the doctor gave him some pills."

"And now?"

"I'm not sure. But he's started following Raynald around again."

"And Martine?"

"She called once or twice during the winter. She went to the Far North to shoot a film about birds, that's all I know."

He got out of his truck to fetch a pail he'd forgotten beside the Virgin Mary.

"I just washed her. I'm going to let her dry before I redo her colours. Believe me, out in the wind like that, she gets pretty beat up in the winter."

I started my engine. I waved to him. Now Martine had left. Over the past few years, the women had been deserting the village. I'd always thought she would be the only one who would never leave. I had never been so wrong about someone.

On my way home, I couldn't separate the image of Martine from that of Jeanne Moreau, as if now that Martine was gone, I'd start to confuse the two.

The Last Coronation

THAT FIRST WINTER, there'd been all those deaths. All the people we used to know in the village. Five of them, I think. I can't remember anymore. I've stopped counting. There were those deaths and Aline, crying at night, her back turned to me, facing the wall. She cried silently, completely immobile. She didn't even blow her nose. I'd been married to her for thirty years and I still can't explain it, but, during those nights, I pretended to be asleep. I didn't have the strength to stroke her shoulder, to turn on the lamp and pass her a Kleenex. I think she started crying the first night we came back. I told myself it would pass, that she was crying because of her sister Régine, because of the wreck that woman had become, and that she'd get over it. When I look back now, I think she cried almost every night she spent in this house, she cried until she left to die in the hospital.

I'm the one who should have died. We left Montreal shortly after my heart attack. The doctor had told me that I had to stop working. We sold our house and we moved into the old barn I'd been fixing up for years. It had become a magnificent old house with exposed beams. Aline was the one who found that term in a book on houses from the French regime. She was always reading, everything she could find, everything people gave her. Here in the village, she had made friends a long time ago with Émile, an old, retired dentist who supplied her with books. He brought them by the boxful, and she returned them once she'd read them. During the summer, they'd sit together in the porch swing and talk about books. She'd make tea. She was crazy about him. She hated the way her sister called Émile an old faggot. Of course, Aline never said anything to her. She never said anything. Aline put up with it. She did the same with me.

Coming back to live in the village was my great idea. I'd been dreaming about it for ages. Every year, I worked on the barn and on the yard, thinking that we'd retire here. It was a big place, we could open a bed and breakfast during the summer months and make a bit of money. Aline used to smile and say we'd see. She must've thought we had lots of time before I'd retire and who knew what would happen. And then, my attack. That upset everything. I can't say I thought I was dying. I didn't have time. I can only remember feeling very weak. I felt like I was in a fog. There was something soft about it. Almost immediately, I felt euphoric. I knew I'd be coming back to the village and nothing else mattered. I spent hours on the phone with my brother-in-law. Despite my convalescence, I was the one who organized everything. We had to sell a lot of our stuff. I spent days making lists. I was on a strict diet. I was losing weight. I hadn't felt so well and light for a long time. I kept thinking, I'm going home, and that was all I could see. Once my daughter said maybe we should keep an apartment in the city for the winter months. She'd be able to see her mother more often and they could still go to the movies together. I shrugged. I said it would cost too much for nothing, and that once we moved to the village, we wouldn't feel like coming back. I was sure of it.

My wife died a year ago. The old dentist is still alive. Last summer, he often came to sit with me at nightfall. He tried to get me to talk. He asked me questions about hunting, about my winter activities, about life in the village when the vacationers are gone. I gave him vague answers. I lied to him about hunting. I didn't tell him that I hadn't gone hunting since my return, that I was waiting to feel stronger before resuming. The first season after we arrived, I spent one day goose hunting and that night, when I got home, I fainted. Aline called her sister to come stay with me and she went to get a doctor who has a country house on the next range line over. She knew he was there, she'd seen his car. He came back with her, examined me and said I no longer had the physical strength to spend entire days out in the cold and the wind.

In all the excitement, we'd forgotten the birds I'd killed on the back porch and in the night or the evening, a dog had torn them apart. We had to throw them out. I stayed cooped up in the house for days. I couldn't imagine myself unable to go hunting again. Even when I was working in Montreal, I always found a way to accumulate enough overtime so I could spend two weeks with my brother and my brother-in-law and bring back a supply of game that ended up with freezer burn, forgotten at the bottom of the freezer. Aline didn't cook game, she said she was incapable. And yet she had been raised in the same village as me. A village where, in the old days, game had certainly saved some families from starvation. Now I can't help but think that this was her way of protesting against my long absence, and all the stories I brought back from the village and kept repeating for months.

When we first moved to Montreal, I lived with a calendar on the refrigerator door, the dates of our stays here circled in red. Actually, I guess I never really left. I dragged the village with me, intact. The village of my youth, not the one where I returned to live. That's why all these deaths are upsetting. Not one of them had a wake, they waited till spring to have the funeral service with the ashes. Our village and the others in the region are served by an old retired priest who doesn't know anyone and who reads anecdotes from *Reader's Digest* instead of a sermon. They are always about acts of charity and miracle cures. During the funerals, Aline kept her head down, embarrassed. No one in the church was listening. Some people even chatted together, like in the funeral parlour. We always came home feeling sad. And it seemed like that was when Aline's sister always chose to visit us.

Régine would arrive in the house, out of breath from extracting herself from her car and smelling strong of sour sweat and alcohol. It was disgusting. She'd become so fat she was incapable of washing herself properly. I'd take advantage of the situation to spend time in my workshop. Aline looked at her, smiled, made some coffee and talked with her, sometimes for hours. After Régine had left, she'd open all the windows. Once I surprised her vomiting in the sink, she hadn't had time to make it to the toilet. Régine made her sick. We never talked about her sister's lack of cleanliness, her monstrous obesity and the way she had raised her children—they all lived with her, none of them was married. They ate in front of the TV, never saying a word to each other. Régine seemed to find that perfectly normal. Her life revolved around the village and nothing else existed. All the parabolic antennas in the world wouldn't have changed a thing, because her life was limited to the village and to the people she had always known here. She managed to ignore the strangers, despite the fact that most of the houses now belonged to rich professional types. Some of the people who have stayed in the village now work for them. I don't like thinking about Aline's sister. It makes me feel ashamed, I'd confined myself to that world, too. She never comes to visit now. She just slows down when she goes by the house in her car.

Ever since Aline's death, I've been collecting old photos taken in the village, most of them portraits. I write the names and dates of birth of the people portrayed. I've even done research on the first inhabitants. People have sent me pictures from as far away as the States. I have more and more of them. They're all over the house. I showed them to the old dentist who was surprised that I was interested in genealogy. He told me they would make a nice book of old photos and I could use them to tell the history of the village. He would help me. I don't know why but I decided that was the only thing I could do with my time. And that's how I spend my days and nights now. Whenever I'm working on it, I talk to Aline, I show her the pictures, explain them to her. They're all over the house with Post-its stuck to them with the names and the dates. I tell myself I'm doing it for her, because she loved books so much. I never go out, except to drive to the next town over for groceries. I don't feel like talking to anyone, I don't have the strength. They all look at me like I'm retarded. I think it's because of the way Aline was buried, they can't get over it. At night, if I have trouble sleeping, I get up and work on my book. It's the only thing that prevents me from thinking about what a castastrophe my life has been since I came back to the village. I can't get rid of the thought that it is to blame for Aline's cancer. She caught the village cancer. Sometimes it seems as if the first two years after we moved back were an unending series of deaths and catastrophes, punctuated by visits from Régine. I should have seen it coming from the very beginning. There were lots of signs.

The first winter, I saw a notice at the grocery store that they had organized a hockey game with the neighbouring town to inaugurate the carnival. It was a beautiful day, I convinced Aline to come with me. When we arrived at the skating rink, all we found was four men who were drinking beer and tossing their empty cans onto the ice. I went up to them, Aline followed me. The game had been cancelled because they hadn't been able to find enough players. It was the second year in a row. They hadn't even shovelled the ice. They said it didn't matter, there'd be the coronation party and everyone from the surrounding villages would be there. We came home without saying a word. The men we had met were all too fat, hardly able to waddle over to their ATVs and they looked exhausted, like old men. That evening, I forced Aline to go out with me again. The whole village was at the hotel. Three young women dressed in sleeveless evening gowns were standing there in a freezing draught, waiting to find out who would be crowned queen of the carnival. They looked unreal. Everyone was wearing snowpants and turtle necks. Most of the people had come by skidoo from the neighbouring villages. Their helmets were on the tables along with the bottles of beer. When the winner was announced, one of the losers ran out screaming it was unfair. Half the crowd rushed over to the window and saw her fall flat on her face in the icy parking lot. The top of her gown came undone. She was screaming. Someone called an ambulance. Everyone watched as they took her away. She was struggling so hard they had trouble strapping her down.

We went back to sit with Régine. She was nursing her vodka and orange juice and kept repeating that it was the cousin of a girl from the next village over and that you could always count on a stranger to make a scene like that. Just because of her, the whole party was spoiled. She was sure this would be the last coronation. The organizers couldn't find enough princesses in the village and nobody attended the activities anymore. This party was the only event people came to and now some crazy bitch had just ruined the evening. Aline told me she wanted to leave. Her sister tried to get her to stay. No, she wouldn't be staying for the buffet. She didn't feel well. That time, too, she vomited when she got home. In the car, she, who never had much to say, told me it was an archaic custom. The word surprised me, but she was right. The following day, on my way to get gas, I saw the carnival queen, walking through town, sporting her tiara instead of a hat. She was wearing a windbreaker and jeans. It must have been minus twenty. The village was deserted, except for her, strolling down the middle of the street. I didn't mention it to Aline.

I told the doctor about her vomiting, later, when they diagnosed Aline's cancer. He told me it was not necessarily a symptom but he couldn't be sure.

I'm not the only one who believes that the village poisoned Aline, my daughter is also convinced of it, even though she has never told me so. When we buried her mother's ashes in the family plot in the middle of the cemetery, she told me that's where it would end, that she wouldn't be buried there. As she was heading back to Montreal just a few hours after the burial, she told me I knew where she lived and that she wouldn't travel six hundred kilometres with a newborn child just to see me or listen to her aunt's dumb comments. She had hidden her pregnancy from her mother. She wanted to spare her that sadness. I don't know if Aline guessed. She never said much, but she knew everything. I haven't seen my daughter since. The baby is due any day now. I haven't spoken with her often either. She thinks I killed her mother by dragging her back here. Maybe she's right.

I can't help but think that Aline died in my place. After my heart attack, I could only think of myself. The village and hunting were all I cared about. Now, when I spend my days sorting my photos, that's what I think about and I talk to her. Aline sacrificed everything. She left the job she loved, she was the secretary in a grade school. She loved the children and it was mutual. She respected her colleagues, the school had always had a good atmosphere and I'm sure Aline contributed to it. I never saw her leave for work in a bad mood. I didn't take anything into consideration, worse than that, it never occurred to me. I had just escaped death and I was going home to my village. Home to the big lake, the mountain and long days of hunting. Back to everything I had missed. That's all I could think of, and I never once thought the village was inhabited by old people and strangers and that the families who had remained there no longer had a social life. There wasn't even a school anymore. The teenagers all went to schools in other towns where they felt like outsiders. On weekends they got stoned and enjoyed destroying everything they could get their hands on. They could see their parents were dependent upon arrogant strangers and that made them violent. Sooner or later, they would drop out. Aline knew all that. When a stranger was murdered in his remote cabin by the mountain, she didn't hesitate for one second, she told me he'd been killed by one of the young people from the village, someone who held something against him. The investigation took more than two years, but she was right, they finally found the murderer. I always wondered how she had guessed. She was so discreet. I'd become accustomed to her silence. It was part of her. I never tried to understand it. I guess it suited me. I made all the decisions and she would smile and say yes. That's how I always knew her and now, I wish she would talk to me, but the old dentist is the only one here to answer me. He had always corresponded with Aline, and when she died, he began to write to me. He sends me books on genealogy, website addresses, tips for my research. He's sure I'll succeed. Sometimes I have the feeling he knows more about Aline and about the village than I do.

He's had a house here for more than forty years and he was the first summer resident. At first, he came with a doctor much older than himself and who spent his days walking on the mountain gathering flowers and pieces of rock. In the fall, he brought medicine that he distributed to the families. I remember my mother used to receive him alone in the sitting room and she'd talk to him for a long time. She would close the door and forbid us to disturb them. She only acted that way with him. For me, he always remained a mystery.

After the doctor's death, the dentist continued to come alone. He'd developed a passion for hunting. He told me the most difficult thing about old age had been to give up hunting, to miss seeing the icy haze over the lake and the flight of birds at dawn, to miss the smell of the damp earth. He adored goose hunting. That really struck me, since I hadn't yet given up hope. I believed and I still believe that I went back too soon after my thrombosis and that I can undoubtedly start again next fall. My guns are hanging on the wall and my hunting clothes are in my workshop, ready for use.

Aline's clothes are still in the bedroom, her toiletry articles are still in the bathroom. I haven't touched a thing. I can't bring myself to do it and, besides, I'm too busy with my project. I still sleep in the guest room. I keep postponing the moment when I'll throw everything into plastic bags and take them to the municipal dump, even if it's forbidden. I refused Régine's offer to help. I didn't want her smell and her paws on Aline's clothes. My daughter didn't take anything, she didn't even consider it. All she wanted was the photo album her mother had been working on for years. There were pictures of her from her baptism up to her university graduation. Aline had written little captions under the photos. *Marie at her graduation ball, age 16. Marie receiving her degree from the principal.* That's where it ended. Aline hadn't had time to sort the most recent pictures.

Throughout her sickness, the trips back and forth from the hospital, the treatments, I never believed for a minute that Aline would die. For me, that was impossible, simply not in the books, not what I had expected at any rate. Both falls when Aline was sick, I didn't bring in my wood, my brother did it for me. He's the one who maintains many of the strangers' houses in the village. He refused to let me pay him. He's the one who set up my winter garage, took out the skidoo, installed the storm windows. In Montreal, we stayed with my daughter. Aline was unhappy to be bedridden, dependent on others and not in her own house. At the end of the second winter, despite all the treatments, the cancer had progressed. She decided to stop everything. I didn't agree, but she insisted. She asked me to take her home. In the beginning, she got up, cooked for us, and then she became too weak. She stayed in bed and read. She didn't want to see anyone, not even her sister. The only visitors she accepted were her daughter and old Émile. Everyone in the village thought she was too proud, that she didn't want them to see her so thin and deteriorated. She was calm and had only one obsession, she wanted to die before winter, before the snow fell. She talked about it constantly with the visiting nurse, who travelled a hundred kilometres round trip to see her. To die before winter. That summer, she ran a fever, her breath was fetid, she was always sucking on mints and she began to complain about her smell. She kept repeating that she smelled bad. She didn't want me to sleep with her. In mid-September, she asked me to drive her to the hospital, the nurse came with us, they set her up in a lilac room reserved for terminal cancer patients who only receive treatment to alleviate their pain. Aline had us arrange all her knickknacks, her vases of dried flowers and she insisted that her bed be made up with white linen. She didn't want a TV, only a radio to listen to music, that was all. She lived for almost another month and she fell into a coma and died quietly, without a spasm or any respiratory distress. It was the first week in October. It was unseasonably hot. In the village, people were complaining that the heat would spoil the hunting season. She was cremated, as she had requested, and there was no funeral. She had insisted she didn't want an obituary notice. My daughter and her husband were the only ones there. The gravedigger waited by his truck. I had the cheque Aline had prepared, I gave it to him immediately. I have never understood her determination to die in such solitude. I had her name added to her mother's gravestone, with her date of birth and date of death. I did everything she requested, even though I didn't agree. She had prepared her last wishes and had stuck them on the fridge door before going into palliative care, exactly like a shopping list.

Yesterday I put part of my work into a box and I went to see the mayor. The old dentist had given me the name of a printer who was used to this kind of publication. They even offered technical advice. I brought some examples of books on villages they had already done and I showed it all to the mayor. I told him it would cost only two or three thousand dollars and we'd get our money back for sure, we could sell it to the tourists during the summer and display it during the Birdwatchers Symposium. I'd said the magic words: money and tourists. He looked at everything, especially the photos of his wife's family. He doesn't come from here himself. He called her to come see. She came down to the basement and spent an hour spreading out all the photos. They were really excited. He'd get a budget approved. I'd have to bring my box to the next town meeting, but he was sure there'd be no problem. When I left, I could hardly wait to get home and send an email to the old dentist. The book would get done, the municipality would find the budget for the printer. That's all I needed. He answered that he was happy and that I could count on him if I needed help. I told Aline she would have her book.

My daughter gave birth to a little boy at the end of March. I went to Montreal for a week. I was uncomfortable, uncomfortable living in such close quarters and besides, I kept worrying about the time I had left to work on my book. The mayor had announced it would be ready for the Birdwatchers Symposium. That gave me less than two months to finish writing and prepare the layout. The printer would come for a few days to help me finalize the presentation. He would stay at Émile's house. I didn't realize at first how exceptional this was, that he was doing it out of friendship for the old man, because he had asked him, and that he had better things to do than waste his time on a small-town publication that wouldn't bring him anything. He had lowered his cost to the bare minimum. He wasn't making any profit.

He arrived one Monday at the end of the day, alone. I'd thought the dentist would come with him. He told me he was unable to come. He was a very tall man with long arms. He seemed very calm, very different from my idea of a printer. He came into the living room, he looked around, there were hundreds of photos spread out all over the place. He said, "It's like a cemetery." He walked around a bit and said we'd make a selection. I showed him my text. He took it with him, it came to about fifty pages that I had written and rewritten, explaining the origin of the village and the historical events, like the fire at the sawmill, the building of the second church. He said, "I'll take it with me, I'll work on it tonight. I'll be back tomorrow. I think that we can finish it in two or three days." On his way out the door, he turned to me and said, "Émile was very fond of your wife, he often spoke of her when he came back in the fall." I didn't answer. I closed the door behind him.

He came back late the following afternoon. He had redone my text and wanted my approval. I couldn't believe it, he had already finished. He said he had a lot of experience. We selected the photos. Without realizing it, I had only chosen ones from the fifties, taken shortly before I left the village. He was the one who said we had to publish some old pictures, too, that's what people are interested in. We numbered them, I wrote the names of the people at the bottom of each picture. We worked until late at night. The printer left with the box containing the book. We'd do the rest by email. The house had never been such a mess. I gathered up the photos any old way and put them in boxes, the printer said we could organize an exhibition, it was worth it. I figured the municipality could make it a summer project.

I went to bed. I couldn't fall asleep. I got up. The snow around the house had almost melted. Ever since Aline died, I hadn't noticed a thing. I couldn't have told you if the winter was rough. I'd locked myself up with the photos of the village. I went into our bedroom for the first time since her death. Everything was in place. I got out some big orange garbage bags, the ones I use for leaves in the fall and I threw everything into them, even the blankets and the pillows from the bed. I put on an old sweater and some shoes and went into my workshop. It was cold. I grabbed my hunting clothes and my boots and threw them in, too. I put everything into the trunk of the car and I headed for the dump.